MISS
MOON

WISE WORDS
from a
DOG GOVERNESS

TO

Finnegan Elliot Woodward,
my beloved Cavalier King Charles spaniel

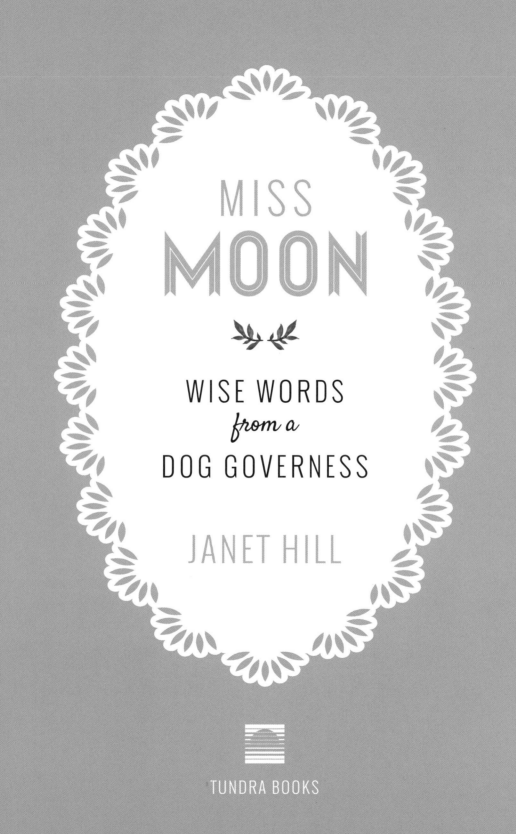

MISS
MOON

WISE WORDS
from a
DOG GOVERNESS

JANET HILL

TUNDRA BOOKS

iss Wilhelmina Moon is a dog governess. Many years ago, she set off with her French bulldog, Petunia, and her monkey, Mitford, to become governess to sixty-seven dogs on an island off the coast of France. It was while Miss Moon was caring for these dogs that she gained the wisdom and skills that make her such a fine governess and excellent companion to her beloved canine charges.

Now Miss Moon wishes to share her knowledge for the good of all dogs and humans. Collected in this volume are Miss Moon's twenty most important lessons for raising happy, healthy, well-mannered pooches — and people.

LESSON
ONE

Friends can come in many shapes and sizes.

LESSON

TWO

Be true to your adventurous spirit.

LESSON

THREE

Respect the property of others.

LESSON
FOUR

Always remember your manners.

LESSON
FIVE

Practice makes perfect.

LESSON

SIX

A good book will chase away the dark.

LESSON

SEVEN

Never stop learning.

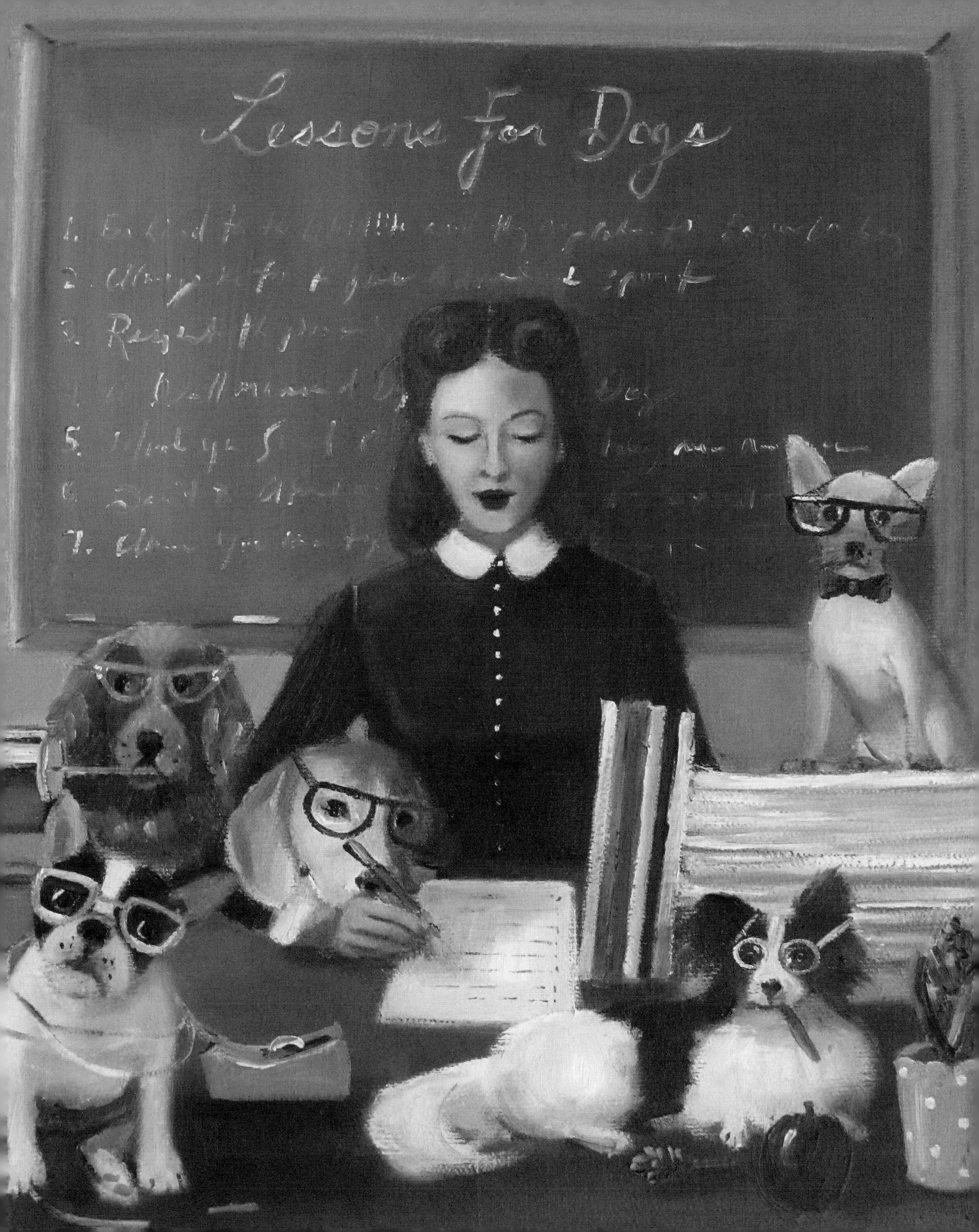
Lessons for Dogs

LESSON

EIGHT

Make-believe is food for the soul.

LESSON
NINE

The impossible can become possible
with a little creativity.

LESSON

TEN

Expect the unexpected.

A tidy space is a welcoming place.

LESSON

TWELVE

Make the most of any weather.

LESSON

THIRTEEN

With a splash of imagination,
anything can be fun.

LESSON
FOURTEEN

Always give the warmest of welcomes.

LESSON

FIFTEEN

Show your loved ones you care.

LESSON

SIXTEEN

Practice the art of conversation:

listen more than you speak.

A good walk is not a race.

Nurture the environment
and you will never be hungry.

Be a good sport and don't be afraid
to get your hair wet.

Celebrate your accomplishments
with family and friends.

CLASS PHOTO

FIFTH ROW FROM LEFT:

Kent, Poncho, Sir Greengrass, Inspector Persil, Pippy,
Pascale, Storm, Minny, Baron Rupert the Third, Jennifer

FOURTH ROW FROM LEFT:

Babette, English Ivy, Polka, Dot, Cowboy Chris, Greenbrier,
Skye, Jupiter, Cora Lace, Valentine, Sister Effie,
Sister Sadie, Sister Bearle, Sister Rose

THIRD ROW FROM LEFT:

Shamrock, Morrison, Penny, Cotton Ball, Goldie, Issac the Wizard, Ira,
Longines, The Count, Shannon, Bumblebee, Kitty

SECOND ROW FROM LEFT:

Nicholas, London, Salt, Olive, Cinnamon, Lemon Drop, Queenie,
Bernie, Greta, Wazoo, Beau Squeaks, Archibald, Wilma

FIRST ROW FROM LEFT:

Heidi, Nelligan, Alvin, Arnold, Whitman, Mademoiselle Violette,
Mr. Bitters, Esmeralda, Rhoda, Petunia, Noon, Daisy,
Finnegan Elliot Woodward, Victor, Neptune, Pearl,
Evelyn Brambles, Cookie, Blanche

Originally published as *Mademoiselle Moon, gouvernante de chiens*
by Les Éditions Marchand de feuilles

Tundra Books, a division of Random House of Canada Limited, a Penguin Random House Company

Library and Archives Canada Cataloguing in Publication

Hill, Janet, 1974–
[Mademoiselle Moon, gouvernante de chiens. English]
Miss Moon, dog governess / by Janet Hill.

Translation of: Mademoiselle Moon, gouvernante de chiens.
Issued in print and electronic formats.
ISBN 978-1-101-91793-0 (bound).–ISBN 978-1-101-91795-4 (epub)

I. Title. II. Title: Mademoiselle Moon, gouvernante de chiens. English.

PS8615.I46M5713 2016   jC843'.6   C2015-901064-0
                                                 C2015-901065-9

Published simultaneously in the United States of America by Tundra Books of Northern New York, a division of Random House of Canada Limited, a Penguin Random House Company

Library of Congress Control Number: 2015931506

English edition edited by Tara Walker and Samantha Swenson
Adapted from an original design by Sarah Scott
The artwork in this book was rendered in oil on canvas.
Stock images: (leaves) © Dreaming Lucy; (doily) © Lana L; both Shutterstock.com.
Case silhouettes: (woman) © Lissabam; (dog) Sergey Yakovlev; both Dreamstime.com;
(linen spine) © pockygallery/Shutterstock.com.
The text was set in Adobe Caslon.
Printed and bound in China

www.penguinrandomhouse.ca

1 2 3 4 5   20 19 18 17 16